Santa's BIG BIG BOOK TO COLOR

A GOLDEN BOOK • NEW YORK

ISBN 0-375-83651-9
www.goldenbooks.com
www.randomhouse.com/kids
PRINTED IN CHINA
10 9 8 7 6 5 4 3 2

Today Is Special!

It's a Poinsettia Day!

"I Know What Day It Is."

"It's Christmas—That's What!"

Let's Sing "Jingle Bells"

And Write Christmas Letters!

Let's Wrap Presents

And Trim the Tree!

"Is Everything Ready?"

Have You Trimmed Your House?

Have You Made Your Snow Man?

Have You Sent Your Cards?

Have You Tied All Your Bows?

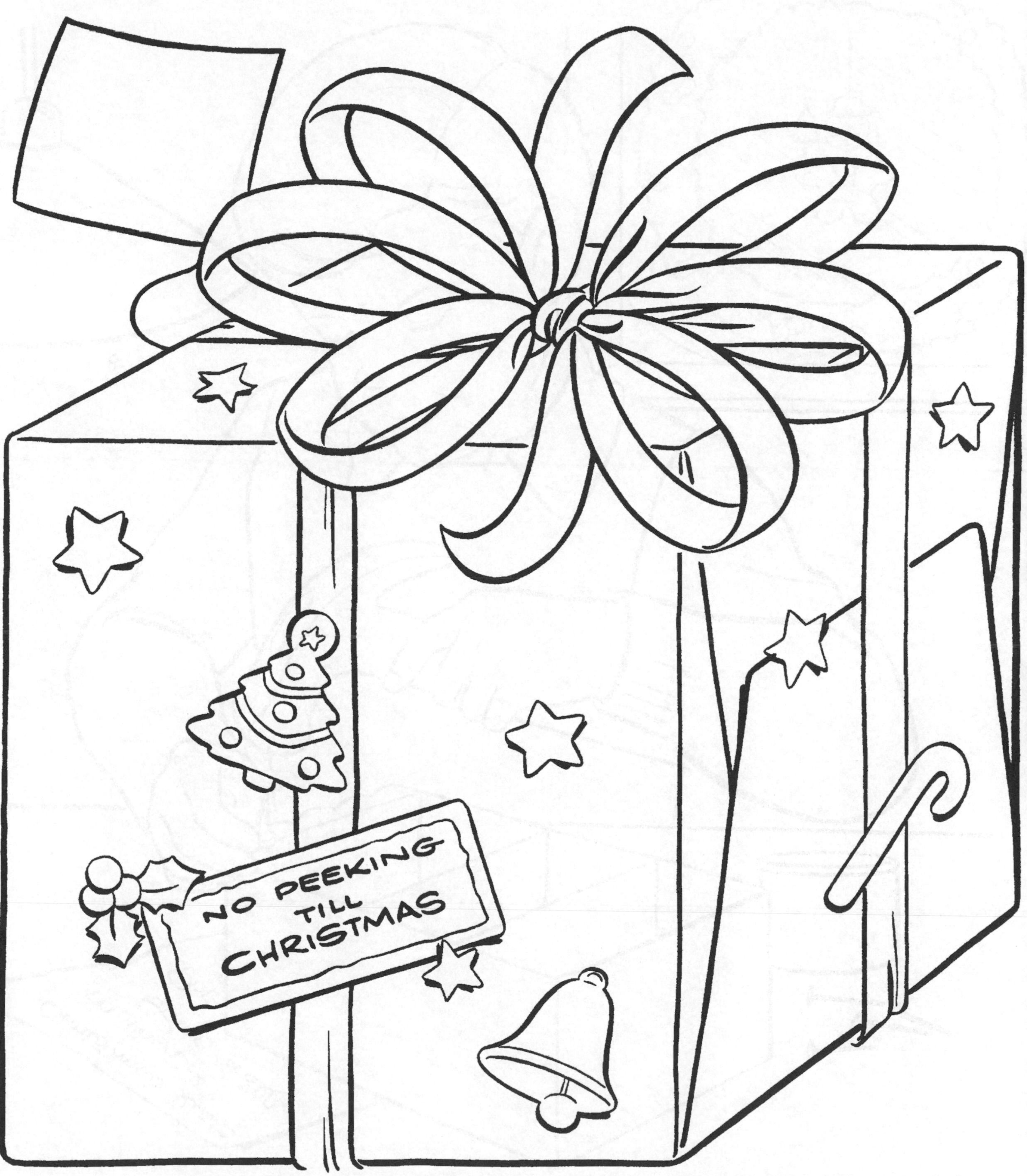
NO PEEKING
TILL
CHRISTMAS

Have You Hidden Your Presents?

Bobby Is Working Hard

He Just Can't Wait!

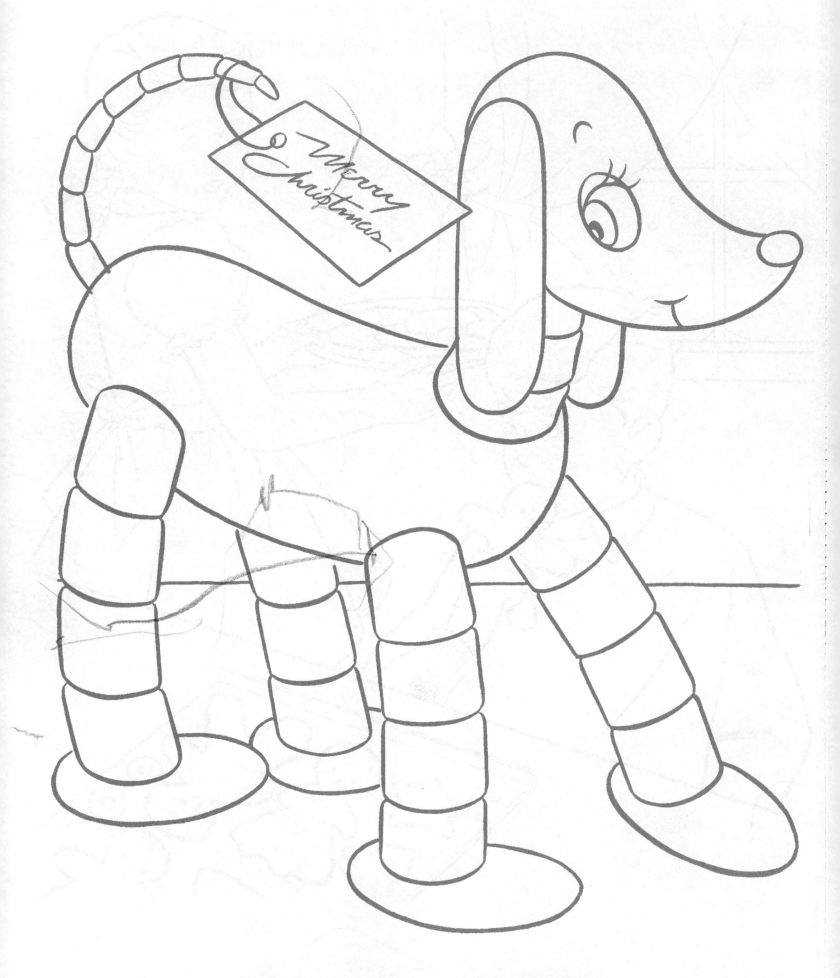

"I'm Ready for Christmas!"

"We're Ready, Too!"

Don't Forget the Birds

Don't Forget Old Snow Man

A Crisp White Coat

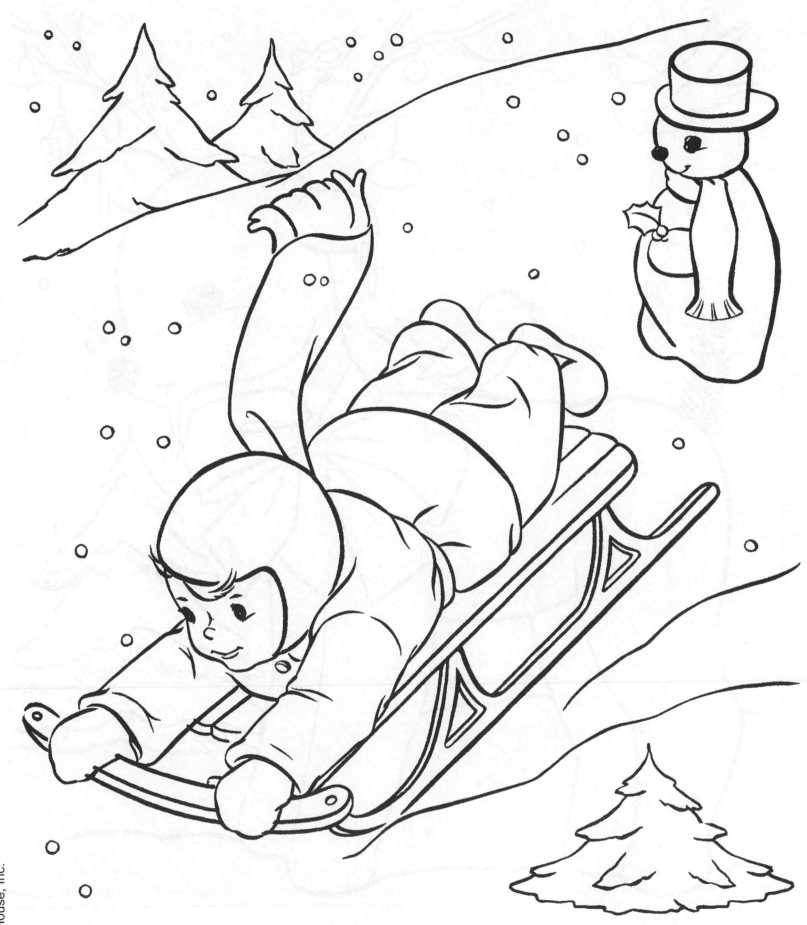

"Look Out! Here I Come!"

Can You Make a Snow Deer?

Can You Make Snow People?

Some Folks Are Sleepy

Some Are Wide Awake

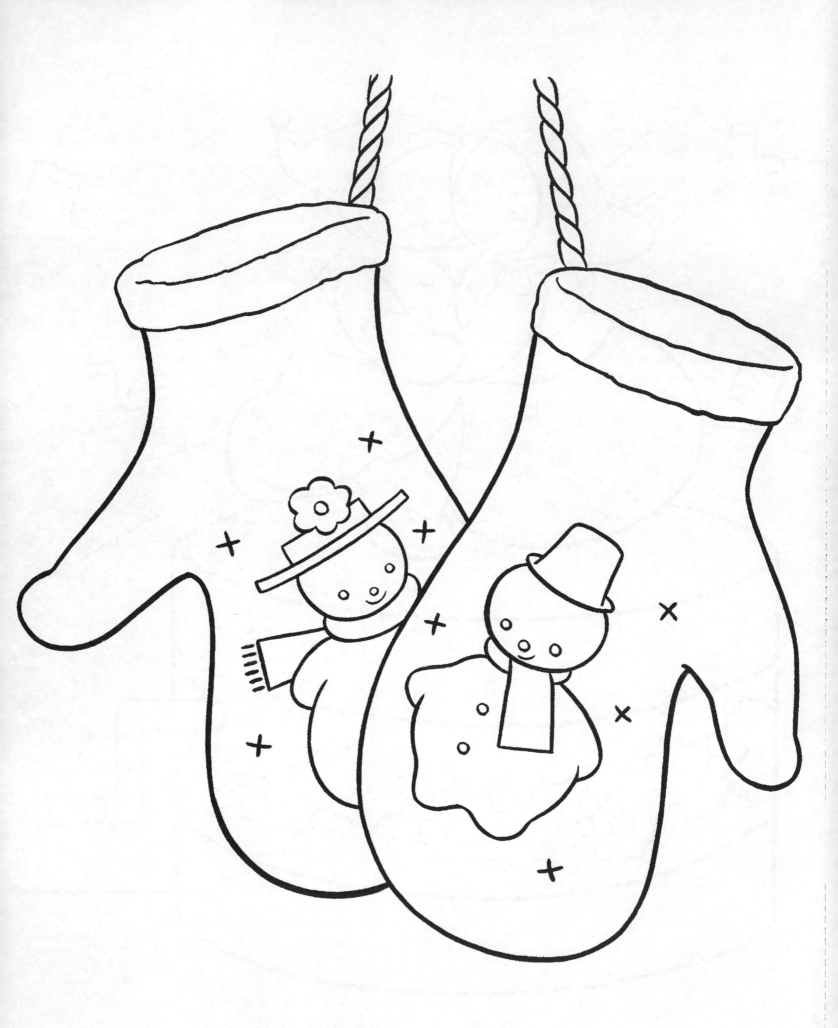

Christmas Mittens for—YOU!

Mrs. Gingerbread Jane

"Hop, Hop, to Santa's House!"

"Everybody Sing!"

"We Help Santa."

"We Help Him Lots!"

We Ring the Big Bells

And We Light the Candles!

We Trim the Windows

Do You Hear Music?

Do You Hear the Singing?

Our Beautiful Tree

Teddy Is Laughing

Jock Is Laughing, Too

A Gingerbread House!

Cookies for Santa Claus

Santa Plays Cowboy

Just for Your Stocking

"How About a Red Nose?"

"I Made Them Myself!"

A Very Special Day!

"Here's Your Surprise!"

Off to Grandma's House

Grandma Bakes Cookies

A Christmas Kitty

Whose Boots Are These?

© Random House, Inc.

Hi, Santa Claus!

"Ho, Ho, Ho!"

Count the Green Candles

Santa Trims the Tree

Hot Sweet Cocoa

And a Christmas Song

"Good Night, Vixen!"

"Mistletoe, Mrs. Santa!"

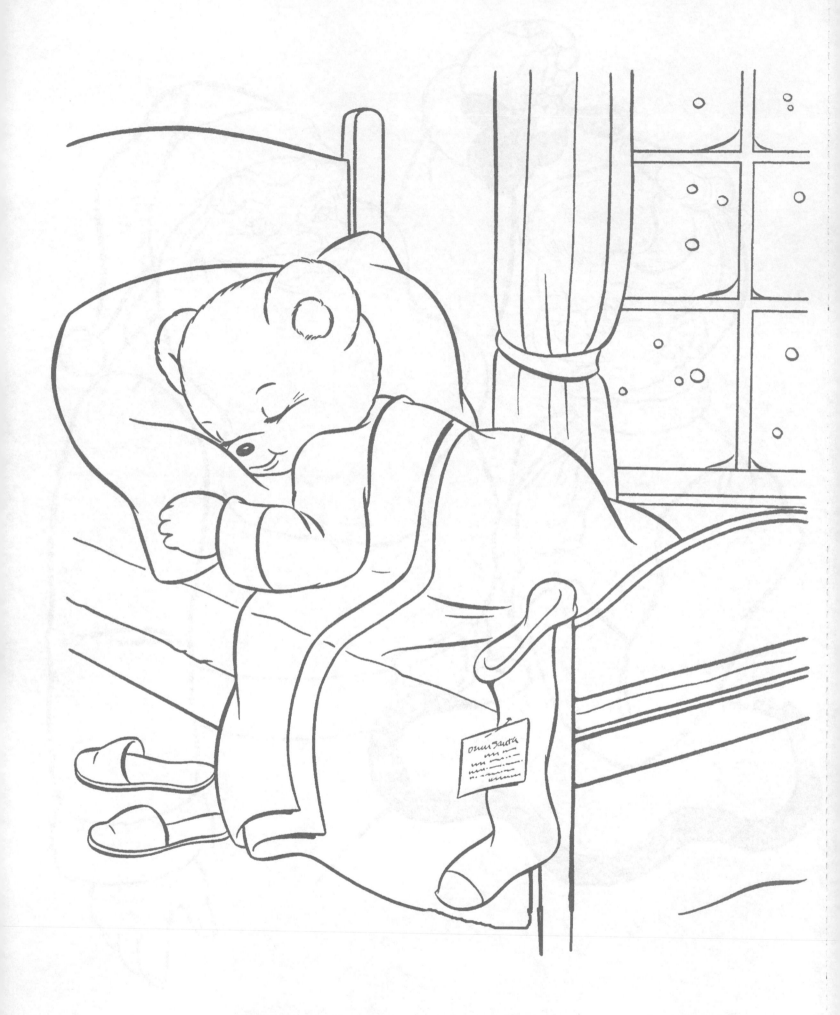

Waiting for Santa to Come

"Here's My Stocking!"

"Tomorrow Is Christmas!"

On the Way to Your House!

Down the Chimney

Whoosh!

"Will Bobby Like This?"

"A Bone for You."

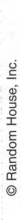

"On, Donner and Blitzen!"

A Whole Bag of Surprises!

"See—He's There!"

"And a Star on Top!"

"Listen—She Talks!"

"My Boots Just Fit!"

"Here's a Bucking Bronco!"

A Red Wagon that Shines

And a Yellow Dog!

Hand Puppets Are Funny

"See You Next Year!"